The Nutcracker

Illustrated by
David Delamare

Adapted from the tale by
E.T.A. Hoffmann

The Unicorn Publishing House, Inc.
Morris Plains, New Jersey

Christmas Eve *had* arrived. The great Christmas tree bore apples of silver and gold, and all its branches were heavy with sugar almonds, bon-bons, and all sorts of delicious things to eat. Along its spreading branches were hundreds of tiny candles, glittering like stars, inviting the children to pluck its flowers and fruit.

The children looked on in wonder, for never before had there been so many beautiful and delightful presents awaiting their eager hands. Marie gazed upon the most beautiful dolls and toys imaginable. Some surrounded the base of the tree while others hung from its branches.

Fritz, her older brother, not content to merely gaze, set at once upon the lovely toys. In no time at all he was at work mustering his troops, a new squadron of hussars. Fritz wanted to whip the troops into shape quickly, so that they might defend the beautiful castle. The castle was a grand sight—a present from their Godpapa Drosselmeier. But *not* the only one.

Amid all the Christmas splendor Marie caught sight of a curious little man hanging quietly from one of the branches, as if patiently waiting his turn to be seen.

As Marie looked at the little man, she began to clearly see a sweet and kind nature in his odd little face. "Oh, Papa," Marie cried at last, "whose present is this little man to be?"

"Well," came the answer, "that little fellow is going to do plenty of good service for all of you." And her papa explained that he was named Nutcracker, for that is what he does best. Then he showed Marie. He took Nutcracker from the tree and lifted the end of the little man's cloak (which was really a handle). Nutcracker opened his mouth, displaying two rows of very white teeth. Then he placed a nut between the little man's teeth and—*crack, crack*—neatly broke the shell. Marie and Fritz clapped their hands with delight.

Fritz grabbed up Nutcracker, and immediately began to misbehave. As Marie watched in horror, Fritz began to stuff nut after nut into Nutcracker's mouth, often forcing nuts that were far too large for the little man to take, until at last—"*CRACK!*" Three teeth fell out of Nutcracker's mouth, and his lower jaw became loose and wobbly.

"Ah! my darling Nutcracker," Marie cried.

"Humph!" said Fritz. "Calls himself a nutcracker, and can't even give a decent bite."

Marie paid no attention to Fritz, and quickly gathered the little man's broken teeth. Taking a ribbon from her dress, she tied it gently around Nutcracker's injured chin. She then cradled Nutcracker in her arms, rocking him to and fro like a child, and whispering words of comfort. When Godpapa Drosselmeier saw the way Marie treated Nutcracker, he laughed at her and complained that she gave far too much attention to such an ugly little man. But Marie continued to soothe her wounded friend.

It was near midnight. Godpapa Drosselmeier had left, and the children were putting all their new toys away in the cupboard. Fritz had bedded down his troops and was ready to do the same for himself. Marie, however, felt there was still quite a bit to do in arranging her new dolls. She begged her parents for a few minutes more. Her parents consented, and the rest of the family went off to bed.

The clock struck midnight. But instead of a bell chime, the clock sounded a dreadful tone. *A warning.* Marie looked up, and saw that the great golden owl which sat on top had moved! The owl had stretched its catlike head and covered the whole of the clock with its wings. The great owl cried out:

> "Clocks, clocks, stop chiming,
> For behind the wall he's hiding;
> Seven wicked heads spit their spite,
> Fourteen eyes burn the night,
> The Mouse-King awaits the twelve to strike,
> When hordes of mice shall show their might."

In the next moment, the owl changed into Godpapa Drosselmeier, and Marie cried out: "Godpapa! Godpapa! Why are you up there? Don't frighten me so!" But there was no reply.

Then they came. Marie heard them before she saw them. She heard the sound of thousands of tiny little feet behind the walls. Marie's heart beat with terror as thousands of mice squeezed through the cracks. The mice crowded together. But the most terrifying thing of all came last—the Mouse-King. The Mouse-King was huge, with seven heads, and upon each head a crown. Each ugly head took its turn and faced the mouse-troop, squeaking out commands. The mouse-army moved forward. Marie fell back against the wall. She was about to scream when her eye caught sight of the cupboard. Every doll and toy soldier was climbing down to meet the mouse-army. And Nutcracker was at the lead. The *battle* had begun.

The fight was fierce. Nutcracker and the army of toys boldly advanced against the mousey horde. Marie watched as her brave Nutcracker fell upon the mouse-troop, delivering one deadly blow after another. But Nutcracker's army was outnumbered by the mice. Little by little, the toys began a retreat.

And then it happened. A clown stumbled, and the mice fell upon him at once. Seeing his comrade fall, Nutcracker bravely fought his way to the clown's side. Marie looked on in horror as Nutcracker was quickly cut off from the rest of the toys. The Mouse-King rushed at him, *squeaking* in triumph out of all his seven throats.

Marie could stand no more. "Oh! my poor Nutcracker!" she sobbed, and taking her left shoe off, she threw it as hard as she could into the mouse-pack, straight at their king.

In an instant *everything* vanished. Marie felt a stinging pain in her arm, and the room began to sway before her eyes. Then everything went black.

When Marie awoke she was lying in her little bed, and the sun was shining brightly through the window. "She's awake," a voice said, and Marie saw the figure of her mother by her bed.

"Oh, Mother!" whispered Marie. "Are all those horrid mice gone, and is Nutcracker safe?"

"Don't talk nonsense, Marie," answered her mother. "What have mice to do with Nutcracker? You must have fallen asleep while playing, and you fell into the cupboard. You cut your arm very badly. Thank heaven, I woke and missed you or you might well have bled to death." At that moment Godpapa Drosselmeier entered the room and came close by Marie's bed.

"Godpapa, how *nasty* you were!" cried Marie. "I saw you quite well sitting on the clock. Why didn't you help Nutcracker? Why didn't you help me? It's your fault I hurt my arm!"

"Why, Marie, what foolishness! How can you talk that way to your godpapa? I don't know what has gotten into you!" her mother scolded.

When Marie's mother left the room, Godpapa Drosselmeier turned to Marie, and said: "Don't be angry with me, Marie, because I didn't kill the Mouse-King. There is far more to this than you know." And he pulled Nutcracker from his pocket, with all his teeth back in their proper place. Marie brightened, and took Nutcracker in her arms.

"Now, let me tell you a story," Godpapa Drosselmeier began, "about how Nutcracker became so ugly. You must admit, Marie, that he is *far* from handsome. But it was not always so. Would you like to hear the story of Nutcracker and Princess Pirlipat?"

"Tell me, Godpapa," Marie cried. "Oh, do tell me!"

THE STORY OF THE HARD NUT

"Did you ever *see* anything so lovely as my little Pirlipat?" boasted the proud king of his new-born daughter. And indeed she was lovely. Princess Pirlipat had been born to a noble king and queen of a small but prosperous country. She brought such joy into the royal house!

One day the king decided a royal feast should be given in honor of his daughter, and that the duty of making the fine puddings and sausages should be undertaken by the queen herself. The queen set at once to her work, browning the pieces of fat that were so important to both dishes. But while she was busy a little voice came to her ears, saying: "Give me some of that fat! I am a *queen* as well as yourself; give it over."

The queen knew who was speaking. It was Dame Mouserink, queen of the mice. The queen was not one to deny a few morsels of browned fat. Dame Mouserink took morsel after morsel of the fine fat and left. But that was not the end of it. Next came her seven sons, then her uncles, then her aunts, then her cousins; all came to take their share. The queen could not stop them and soon found herself with only a little fat left with which to make her puddings and sausages. Far too little. The dishes were ruined, making the king furious. He ordered that all the mice in the palace be killed. Traps were set. First Dame Mouserink's seven sons were killed, then her uncles, then her aunts, and then her cousins. In rage and despair, Dame Mouserink fled. The royal court rejoiced. The queen, however, was very much afraid of what Dame Mouserink might do.

Late one evening, Dame Mouserink came. The queen of the mice cried an angry curse, saying: "My sons and my uncles, my cousins and my aunts, are no more. Have a care, lady, lest I bite *your* little princess in two! Have a care, I say!" And she vanished.

On that night, and for every night after, great precautions were taken to see to the princess's safety. Six nurses sat, with six cats, around Princess Pirlipat's cradle. They kept watch all night, waiting for Dame Mouserink to come. One night a cry arose from one of the nurses as she saw a hideous mouse, standing on its hind legs, upon the face of the princess! She sprang up with a scream of terror! Everyone dashed for Dame Mouserink, but it was too late! She was off and away through a crack in the floor. The noise woke Pirlipat, who cried terribly. "Heaven be thanked, she is still alive!" cried the nurses. But as they peered into the cradle and beheld the princess, moans of sorrow went up. For there lay not the beautiful blue-eyed child that they loved so dearly, but a horribly deformed thing. Pirlipat now had an enormous head and a little crumpled-up body. Green, wooden-like eyes stared out blankly, and her mouth had stretched across from one ear to the other! Dame Mouserink had her revenge. Sorrow spread through the land for poor Pirlipat. *What* could be done?

The Court Astronomer was called upon to discover a cure. He consulted the stars. To assist him he had a great friend by the name of Drosselmeier (who also happened to look just like Godpapa), and they were at work for three days and three nights before they had an answer. The cure seemed simple enough. To return the princess to her former beauty she must eat the sweet kernel of the *nut* Crackatook.

But there were problems. The Crackatook nut is the hardest nut in all the world. Moreover, it was essential that the nut be cracked, in the princess's presence, by the teeth of a young man whose beard had never known a razor. The young man must crack the nut and hand the kernel over to the princess, always keeping his eyes closed, and he could not open them again till he had taken seven steps backwards without stumbling. The two friends set off at once to find the nut.

For twenty years they traveled in search of the nut, without even a clue as to where one lay hidden. They had many adventures, far too many to recount here, but at last they returned home—empty handed.

But when they walked through the door, Drosselmeier's cousin was waiting there for them, and ran up saying: "Oh my, you have been gone a long time, cousin! I have the nut! One was given to me many years ago as a present. Here!" And the cousin produced a small nut inscribed with Chinese characters.

"This is it! This is it!" cried the Astronomer. Now the two need only find the young man. But where? Again the cousin came to the rescue. "You must see my son! He is the one, I tell you!" And the young man was sent for at once.

He appeared at the door dressed in a beautiful red coat with gold trimmings, a sword by his side, and a fine wig with a pigtail. He was very good-looking, and often kept himself amused by cracking nuts for the young ladies in town, who called him "the handsome nutcracker."

"This is the very man!—we have him!—he is found!" they cried. They made for the palace at once. Many had tried over the years to cure the princess; but all had failed. The king proclaimed that the man who could lift Dame Mouserink's curse would have Princess Pirlipat as his bride. The handsome nutcracker stepped forward with the nut. Princess Pirlipat was impressed with the good-looking fellow. The young man closed his eyes and bit hard into the nut. "*CRACK!*" He gave the sweet kernel to Pirlipat and began to take the seven steps backwards. With each step the princess became more and more her beautiful self. But just as he was about to take the seventh step, Dame Mouserink came from hiding and ran under the poor fellow's foot. He stumbled. In the next instant the handsome nutcracker was *transformed*.

The young man lay there, looking exactly as the princess had before. Dame Mouserink lay there, too, having been crushed underfoot. She lifted her head up and said with a feeble voice: "Peep peep, woe's me, I cry!—since by the hard nut I must die.—But, brave young Nutcracker, I see—you soon must follow me.—My sweet young son, with sevenfold crown—will soon bring Master Cracker down.—His mother's death he will repay—so, Nutcracker, *beware* that day!" And she died.

When the princess, now quite beautiful, saw the ugly young man, she turned away in disgust. The king said he would never allow his daughter to marry such a horrid-looking fellow and banished Nutcracker from his kingdom. That *was* the hero's reward! And it is said that Nutcracker will always remain ugly until a beautiful girl gives her love to him—for only she shall see the true beauty that lies in his heart. But until that day, Nutcracker must be wary—for the Mouse-King seeks his revenge.

Thus ended Godpapa Drosselmeier's story.

Marie had to spend several days in bed while her injured arm healed. When she was finally allowed to leave her bed, Marie went straight to the cupboard to see Nutcracker. There he was, standing proud, alongside all the other toys.

Was Godpapa's story true? Was Nutcracker *really* under a spell? Or was the fight with the Mouse-King only a dream? Everything in the cupboard was quiet and still. Marie thought Princess Pirlipat a very nasty thing for not having loved Nutcracker after all he had suffered for her. Twilight fell, and Marie went back to bed.

Far into the night, as the moon shone bright, Marie was awakened by a curious noise. In one corner of the room a sound arose, as if small stones were being thrown, followed by the horrid noises of cheeping and squeaking. The *mice* had returned.

Marie sat up in bed. The noise suddenly stopped. Marie couldn't move a muscle—for she saw the king of the mice working himself out through a hole in the wall. Once inside, he ran about the room, came to a halt, then with one giant leap was up on the little table beside Marie's bed.

"Hee-hehee!" he cried. "Give me your candy! Do as I say! Out with your cakes, your sugar-sticks, your gingerbread! Don't pause to argue! For if you don't do as I say, I'll *chew* Nutcracker to pieces. Just see if I don't!" As the Mouse-King continued to squeak out his vile threats, Marie hurried to gather up candy. Placing the candy on the little table, Marie watched with horror as the seven greedy mouths set upon her sugary treats. As three of the Mouse-King's heads gnawed at the candy, the other four snarled at Marie, saying: "Give me your sugar treats; give them you must, or else I'll chew Nutcracker up into dust! Tee-hee hehee!" Then he was gone. It *wasn't* a dream. It was all true. Marie put her face in her pillow and wept.

Night after night the Mouse-King came. And night after night he demanded more and more from poor Marie. He ate all of her sugar toys, her cakes, her chocolate bon-bons, and her sugar-sticks. Nothing was left. Marie's father set traps to catch the mice; but the Mouse-King was far too clever for that.

One night Marie woke to find something cold and heavy climbing on her arm. The Mouse-King placed his wet nose near her ear, hissing: "Hee-he, my dear, I am here!—Happy to see me—to be *oh* so near!—You thought the trap might catch some prey!—Some mousey death to come this day?—No, my dear, that will not be!—The king of mice still runs free!" He demanded that she give over all her new dresses and all her new books, so that he might tear them to shreds. Then he jumped to the floor, saying he would soon return for what was his. Marie was beside herself with fright, and wept bitterly.

But in time Marie began to gather her dresses and books together for the Mouse-King. She just couldn't let him destroy Nutcracker. As she placed her precious things in a pile, a sound arose from outside her door. There was a rustling and a clanging- and suddenly there came a shrill "Squeak!" The king of the mice had returned, Marie thought. Everything was silent; but soon there came a gentle tapping at the door, and a soft voice called out: "Please open the door, my dear Marie. Don't be alarmed. It is I, Nutcracker, and I have good news."

Marie ran to open the door. There stood Nutcracker, with his sword covered with blood in his left hand, and a little wax candle in his right. When he saw Marie, he knelt down on one knee. With a gentle *bow* of his head, he placed before her the seven crowns of the Mouse-King.

"I have at long last defeated my enemy," Nutcracker began, "because you, Marie, gave me the strength to do so. I could not allow you to give up your most precious things to keep me from harm. Your courage has become *my* courage. And now, if you will let me, I would like to take you to a very special place."

They had only to walk into Marie's little closet to enter the world of Nutcracker. The first thing Marie noticed was that Nutcracker was almost her size. Had he grown or had she shrunk? They stood looking out across a lovely, sweet-scented meadow.

Nutcracker beckoned Marie to follow, and soon they found themselves in a most delightful forest. "This is known as Christmas Wood," said Nutcracker. The leaves and branches of the wood were made of gold leaf and glittered in the night sky. Silver tinsel hung down from the branches, piping a delicate tune as they *rustled* in the wind. Thousands of sparkling lights rose with the music, eager to join the dance.

Nutcracker clapped his little hands, and there appeared a number of tiny people, as white and delicate as pure sugar. They brought a golden chair, and invited Marie to sit. Then they performed a pretty ballet for her, moving as one to the music of the wood. When they had finished, Nutcracker took Marie by the hand and led her out of the forest.

"We must keep moving," Nutcracker said, "for there is a great deal I wish to show you before this night is through."

As they walked along, they saw many beautiful things. They passed the Honey River and the Orange Brook. They saw many small towns and villages; some made of lemon peels and almond shells, and even one made of pure chocolate. But at last they came to the shore of a beautiful lake, rosy-red and fragrant, a shining water on which shone silver waves that tossed to and fro. In between the falling crests glided snow-white swans, murmuring an *ancient* song. This was Lake Rosa.

There was a boat in the shape of a swan to meet them, pulled by seven shining dolphins. They departed. As they moved across the water the dolphins sang with silvery voices, sending streams of crystal water high in the air from their nostrils, which fell down in glittering, sparkling rainbows.

Marie was delighted by the vision before her, and bent over the boat to gaze at the rippling water below. There she saw a reflection. But it was not her face that looked up from the sweet water. It was the face of Princess Pirlipat!

Nutcracker sighed, and said: "Do not be alarmed, Marie; it is only *yourself*, always *your* own lovely face smiling up from the rosy waves." Marie was embarrassed, and sat back quickly. But as she looked up she saw the most beautiful sight of all. For there on the shore rose a magnificent castle made entirely of candy. This was Marzipan Castle. This was Nutcracker's home.

They arrived by a golden carriage to the castle steps. There they were greeted by pearl-headed pages whose garments were woven gems. They were led into a great hall where a banquet was being held. As they walked past the people who had gathered for the feast, each one turned and bowed. Nutcracker pointed to the end of the hall, where two beautiful thrones sat side by side. Nutcracker was speaking, but Marie couldn't understand him. Everything began to sway and blur before her eyes. She felt as if she were falling away—far, far away. And then came a crash and a tumble! Then *silence*.

Marie woke to find herself in her own bed! It was daylight, and her mother was standing at her bedside, saying: "Well, what a sleep you have had! Breakfast has been ready for ever so long." What had happened? Had she only dreamed of the Marzipan Castle? No! It *was* real! Nutcracker was real! Marie knew in her heart it was all true. But no one believed her. Not even Godpapa Drosselmeier would listen to her. She showed him the seven crowns of the Mouse-King, but still he denied everything! Why?

Years passed, but Marie still believed. Nutcracker had stood silent through the years, not even once uttering a word. One day, when Godpapa Drosselmeier was visiting, Marie took Nutcracker in her arms, and without even knowing quite what she was saying, she whispered softly: "Ah, my dear Nutcracker, if you *really* were alive, I shouldn't be like Princess Pirlipat and despise you. I would have loved you for giving all for my sake!"

Godpapa Drosselmeier turned to Marie and said "Nonsense," but she could clearly see the old man was smiling. Why, Godpapa looked as if he would burst open with joy at any moment!

The very next day a knock came at the door. It was Godpapa Drosselmeier. And with him was a very handsome young gentleman. His little face was red and white; he had on a beautiful red coat trimmed with gold lace and a sword by his side, and he wore his hair neatly back in a pigtail. He held in his hands a lovely bouquet of flowers, which he offered to Marie. Godpapa introduced the young man as his nephew, who had long been away. Too long.

When Marie and the young man were left to visit alone for a while, he spoke to her: "Ah, my beloved Marie, it is I, Nutcracker, whose life you *saved* here on this very spot!"

Marie was stunned, for she understood what her godpapa had told her so long ago. For within the cupboard were many fine dolls—but Nutcracker was gone!

"You see," the young man began, "that Nutcracker is no longer. For you were kind enough to say that you would not have despised me, as Princess Pirlipat did, if I had been turned ugly for your sake. I have ceased to be Nutcracker and have been returned to my former self. Because of you I live again!" And kneeling on one knee, with a gentle *bow* to his head, he asked her hand in marriage.

When a year and a day had passed, the marriage took place. And they say that he came and fetched her away in a golden coach, drawn by a silver horse, to the Marzipan Castle. There they reign, as king and queen, with *joy* forevermore.

For over a decade, Unicorn has been publishing
richly illustrated editions of classic and contemporary
works for children and adults. To continue this tradition,
WE WOULD LIKE TO KNOW WHAT YOU THINK.

If you would like to send us your suggestions or obtain
a list of our current titles, please write to:
THE UNICORN PUBLISHING HOUSE, INC.
P.O. Box 377
Morris Plains, NJ   07950
ATT: Dept CLP

Printing History 15 14 13 12 11 10 9 8 7 6 5 4 3 2

Library of Congress Cataloging-in-Publication Data

The Nutcracker / illustrated by David Delamare ; adapted from the tale by
E.T.A. Hoffmann.
p. cm.
Summary: After hearing how her toy nutcracker got his ugly face, a little
girl helps break the spell and changes him into a handsome prince.
[1. Fairy tales.] I. Delamare, David, ill. II. Hoffmann, E.T.A. (Ernst
Theodor Amadeus), 1776-1822. Nussknacker und Mausekönig.
English.
PZ8.N94 1991
[E]—dc20   91-2167
                                                            CIP
                                                            AC